Hello, my name is Alex. I am a dinosaur.

I love to eat **B**ananas dipped into chocolate or **C**arrot **C**ake.

On **D**ay 6, God created me,
and other land animals, like **E**lephants!

I live in a new garden filled with good **F**ruit,

with all kinds of animals like noisy Goats, tall Giraffes,

fast cheetahs, white Horses, tiny mice, and pretty peacocks.

God made my friend Riley. She loves Ice cream.

She loves to **J**ump. She is very **K**ind.
She likes to **L**ick butterflies.

After God made us He made Man. We lived together in the garden.

The man's Name was Adam.

God let Adam name all the animals. He named **O**ld ostriches and pretty **P**arrots.

He named *other* birds **Q**uail. He named a *long-eared* animal **R**abbit. He named me Be-he-moth, but my friends call me Alex.

Adam **S**at all by himself, and God took one of his ribs to make Eve.

There were fun things to do in the Garden full of Trees.

We would pick **U**p fruit when it fell from the trees. We played tag, but the **V**ulture, **W**olf or cheetah always won. They are very fast. We played hide-n-seek with the fo**X**. The leopard was hard to find with his black spots.

I was happy just eating **Y**ellow bananas dipped in chocolate.
Yes, I ate *too* many... again!

Our garden was like a beautiful Zoo with all of God's animals.

One day Riley and I saw Eve talk to the serpent at a special tree.
God had told Adam they were not to eat from that tree.

She did not do what God said. Adam and Eve both ate the fruit.

God punished them, and they were sent out of the garden.

After that, it was not as much fun in the Garden.

One day I dipped my banana in what looked like chocolate, and ate mud-dipped bananas.

Riley and I learned that God is powerful. He created everything. We should do our best to please and always obey God.